THIS BOOK

BELONGS TO:

....

....

THE TALE OF
Mrs. Tiggy-Winkle

THE TALE OF
MRS. TIGGY-WINKLE

BY

BEATRIX POTTER

A PETER RABBIT™

110th Anniversary Edition

FREDERICK WARNE

FOR THE

REAL LITTLE LUCIE OF NEWLANDS

FREDERICK WARNE

Published by the Penguin Group
Penguin Books Ltd., 80 Strand, London WC2R 0RL, England
Penguin Group (USA) Inc., 375 Hudson Street, New York, New York 10014, USA
Penguin Group (Australia), 250 Camberwell Road, Camberwell,
Victoria 3124, Australia (a division of Pearson Australia Group Pty. Ltd.)
Penguin Group (Canada), 90 Eglinton Avenue East, Suite 700, Toronto,
Ontario M4P 2Y3, Canada (a division of Pearson Penguin Canada Inc.)
Penguin Books India Pvt. Ltd., 11 Community Centre, Panchsheel Park, New Delhi—110 017, India
Penguin Group (NZ), 67 Apollo Drive, Rosedale, Auckland 0632,
New Zealand (a division of Pearson New Zealand Ltd.)
Penguin Books (South Africa) (Pty.) Ltd, 24 Sturdee Avenue, Rosebank, Johannesburg 2196, South Africa

Penguin Books Ltd., Registered Offices: 80 Strand, London WC2R 0RL, England

Website: www.peterrabbit.com

First published by Frederick Warne in 1905
First published with reset text and new reproductions
of Beatrix Potter's illustrations in 2002
This edition published in 2011

001 - 10 9 8 7 6 5 4 3 2 1

New reproductions copyright © Frederick Warne & Co., 2002
Original copyright in text and illustrations © Frederick Warne & Co., 1905
Frederick Warne & Co. is the owner of all rights, copyrights and trademarks
in the Beatrix Potter character names and illustrations.

Colour reproduction by
EAE Creative Colour Ltd, Norwich
Printed and bound in China

PUBLISHER'S NOTE

In the spring of 1904, Beatrix Potter determined that one of her publications for 1905 would be her 'hedgehog book'. This was in spite of the doubts expressed by her editor (and soon to be fiancé) Norman Warne of Frederick Warne & Co., over whether such an unusual animal would make a popular children's book.

'I think "Mrs. Tiggy" would be all right,' Beatrix responded. 'It is a girl's book ... there must be a large audience of little girls. I think they would like the different clothes.'

This argument eventually won over Warne, but neither author nor editor were quite right. In the book itself, both the clothes and the little-girl character Lucie are merely an accompaniment to the wonderful Mrs. Tiggy-winkle herself, who has come to enjoy enormous popularity over the years.

ONCE UPON A TIME there was a little girl called Lucie, who lived at a farm called Little-town. She was a good little girl — only she was always losing her pocket-handkerchiefs!

One day little Lucie came into the farm-yard crying — oh, she did cry so! "I've lost my pocket-handkin! Three handkins and a pinny! Have *you* seen them, Tabby Kitten?"

THE kitten went on washing her white paws; so Lucie asked a speckled hen—

"Sally Henny-penny, have *you* found three pocket-handkins?"

But the speckled hen ran into a barn, clucking—

"I go barefoot, barefoot, barefoot!"

AND then Lucie asked Cock Robin sitting on a twig.

Cock Robin looked sideways at Lucie with his bright black eye, and he flew over a stile and away.

Lucie climbed upon the stile and looked up at the hill behind Little-town—a hill that goes up—up—into the clouds as though it had no top!

And a great way up the hill-side she thought she saw some white things spread upon the grass.

Lucie scrambled up the hill as fast as her short legs would carry her; she ran along a steep path-way — up and up — until Little-town was right away down below — she could have dropped a pebble down the chimney!

PRESENTLY she came to a spring, bubbling out from the hill-side.

Some one had stood a tin can upon a stone to catch the water — but the water was already running over, for the can was no bigger than an egg-cup! And where the sand upon the path was wet — there were foot-marks of a *very* small person.

Lucie ran on, and on.

THE path ended under a big rock. The grass was short and green, and there were clothes-props cut from bracken stems, with lines of plaited rushes, and a heap of tiny clothes pins — but no pocket-handkerchiefs!

But there was something else — a door! straight into the hill; and inside it some one was singing —

"Lily-white and clean, oh!
    With little frills between, oh!
        Smooth and hot — red rusty spot
    Never here be seen, oh!"

LUCIE knocked — once — twice, and interrupted the song. A little frightened voice called out "Who's that?"

Lucie opened the door: and what do you think there was inside the hill? — a nice clean kitchen with a flagged floor and wooden beams — just like any other farm kitchen. Only the ceiling was so low that Lucie's head nearly touched it; and the pots and pans were small, and so was everything there.

THERE was a nice hot singey smell; and at the table, with an iron in her hand, stood a very stout short person staring anxiously at Lucie.

Her print gown was tucked up, and she was wearing a large apron over her striped petticoat. Her little black nose went sniffle, sniffle, snuffle, and her eyes went twinkle, twinkle; and underneath her cap — where Lucie had yellow curls — that little person had PRICKLES!

"Who are you?" said Lucie. "Have you seen my pocket-handkins?"

The little person made a bob-curtsey — "Oh yes, if you please'm; my name is Mrs. Tiggy-winkle; oh yes if you please'm, I'm an excellent clear-starcher!" And she took something out of a clothes-basket, and spread it on the ironing-blanket.

"WHAT's that thing?" said Lucie—
"that's not my pocket-handkin?"

"Oh no, if you please'm; that's a little scarlet waist-coat belonging to Cock Robin!"

And she ironed it and folded it, and put it on one side.

THEN she took something else off a clothes-horse —

"That isn't my pinny?" said Lucie.

"Oh no, if you please'm; that's a damask table-cloth belonging to Jenny Wren; look how it's stained with currant wine! It's very bad to wash!" said Mrs. Tiggy-winkle.

MRS. TIGGY-WINKLE's nose went sniffle, sniffle, snuffle, and her eyes went twinkle, twinkle; and she fetched another hot iron from the fire.

"There's one of my pocket-handkins!" cried Lucie — "and there's my pinny!"

Mrs. Tiggy-winkle ironed it, and goffered it, and shook out the frills.

"Oh that *is* lovely!" said Lucie.

"AND what are those long yellow things with fingers like gloves?"

"Oh, that's a pair of stockings belonging to Sally Henny-penny — look how she's worn the heels out with scratching in the yard! She'll very soon go barefoot!" said Mrs. Tiggy-winkle.

"Why, there's another handkersniff—but it isn't mine; it's red?"

"Oh no, if you please'm; that one belongs to old Mrs. Rabbit; and it *did* so smell of onions! I've had to wash it separately, I can't get out the smell."

"There's another one of mine," said Lucie.

"WHAT are those funny little white things?"

"That's a pair of mittens belonging to Tabby Kitten; I only have to iron them; she washes them herself."

"There's my last pocket-handkin!" said Lucie.

"AND what are you dipping into the basin of starch?"

"They're little dicky shirt-fronts belonging to Tom Tit-mouse — most terrible particular!" said Mrs. Tiggy-winkle. "Now I've finished my ironing; I'm going to air some clothes."

"What are these dear soft fluffy things?" said Lucie.

"Oh, those are woolly coats belonging to the little lambs at Skelghyl."

"Will their jackets take off?" asked Lucie.

"Oh yes, if you please'm; look at the sheep-mark on the shoulder. And here's one marked for Gatesgarth, and three that come from Little-town. They're *always* marked at washing!" said Mrs. Tiggy-winkle.

AND she hung up all sorts and sizes of clothes — small brown coats of mice; and one velvety black mole-skin waist-coat; and a red tail-coat with no tail belonging to Squirrel Nutkin; and a very much shrunk blue jacket belonging to Peter Rabbit; and a petticoat, not marked, that had gone lost in the washing — and at last the basket was empty!

Then Mrs. Tiggy-winkle made tea—a cup for herself and a cup for Lucie. They sat before the fire on a bench and looked sideways at one another. Mrs. Tiggy-winkle's hand, holding the tea-cup, was very very brown, and very very wrinkly with the soap-suds; and all through her gown and her cap, there were *hair-pins* sticking wrong end out; so that Lucie didn't like to sit too near her.

WHEN they had finished tea, they tied up the clothes in bundles; and Lucie's pocket-handkerchiefs were folded up inside her clean pinny, and fastened with a silver safety-pin.

And then they made up the fire with turf, and came out and locked the door, and hid the key under the door-sill.

THEN away down the hill trotted Lucie and Mrs. Tiggy-winkle with the bundles of clothes!

All the way down the path little animals came out of the fern to meet them; the very first that they met were Peter Rabbit and Benjamin Bunny!

AND she gave them their nice clean clothes; and all the little animals and birds were so very much obliged to dear Mrs. Tiggy-winkle.

So that at the bottom of the hill when they came to the stile, there was nothing left to carry except Lucie's one little bundle.

LUCIE scrambled up the stile with the bundle in her hand; and then she turned to say "Good-night," and to thank the washer-woman. — But what a *very* odd thing! Mrs. Tiggy-winkle had not waited either for thanks or for the washing bill!

She was running running running up the hill — and where was her white frilled cap? and her shawl? and her gown — and her petticoat?

AND *how* small she had grown—
and *how* brown — and covered
with PRICKLES!

Why! Mrs. Tiggy-winkle was
nothing but a HEDGEHOG.

*

(Now some people say that little Lucie had
been asleep upon the stile — but then how
could she have found three clean pocket-
handkins and a pinny, pinned with a silver
safety-pin?

And besides — *I* have seen that door into
the back of the hill called Cat Bells — and
besides *I* am very well acquainted with dear
Mrs. Tiggy-winkle!)

THE END